Adapted from the animated film created by Chris Wedge

Bunny

ipicturebooks

New York
www.ipicturebooks.com
Distributed by Little, Brown and Company

JUL   2002

ipicturebooks.com
24 W. 25th St.
New York, NY 10010

Visit us at **ipicturebooks.com**

Library of Congress Cataloging-in-Publication Data available
TWP
Printed in Singapore

One night as Bunny sifted
and stirred, she heard a noise.

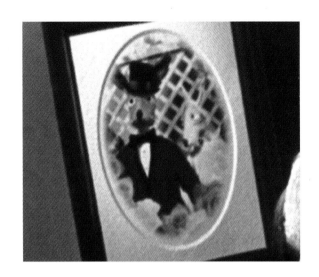

A careless moth had hit Bunny's favorite picture, a photo from her wedding.

Bunny was annoyed. She put the moth out on the porch and turned out the light.

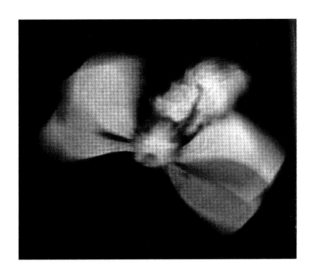

Later, Bunny was grating and mixing.
She heard the sound of wings beating
against the screen.

Bunny went to investigate, but the
night was quiet, and she saw nothing.

When Bunny went back to her baking,
the moth swooped in.

Darting here and there, the moth flew
a curvy path through the kitchen. Now
Bunny was angry.

And with one precise swing of her spoon,
she hit the moth.
It fell into the cake batter.

Bunny stopped. She was out of breath.
Then she mixed the moth, furiously,
into the batter.

She poured the batter into the pan.
She put the pan into the oven.
And she slammed the door shut.

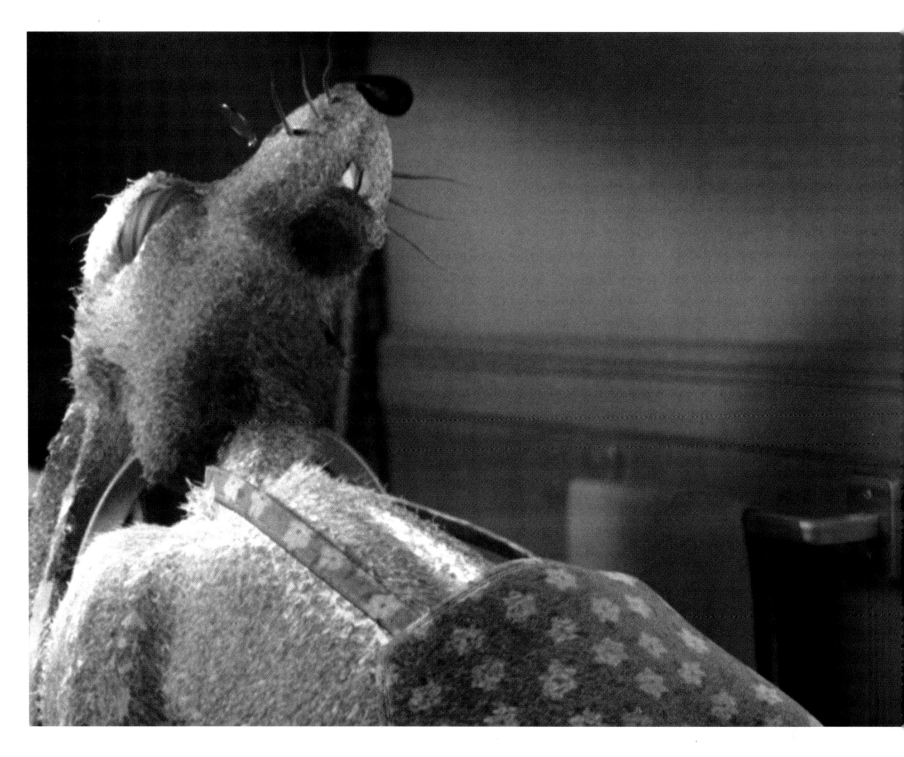

As the cake baked, Bunny fell asleep.

Suddenly the stove started to glow. The dishes began to rattle.

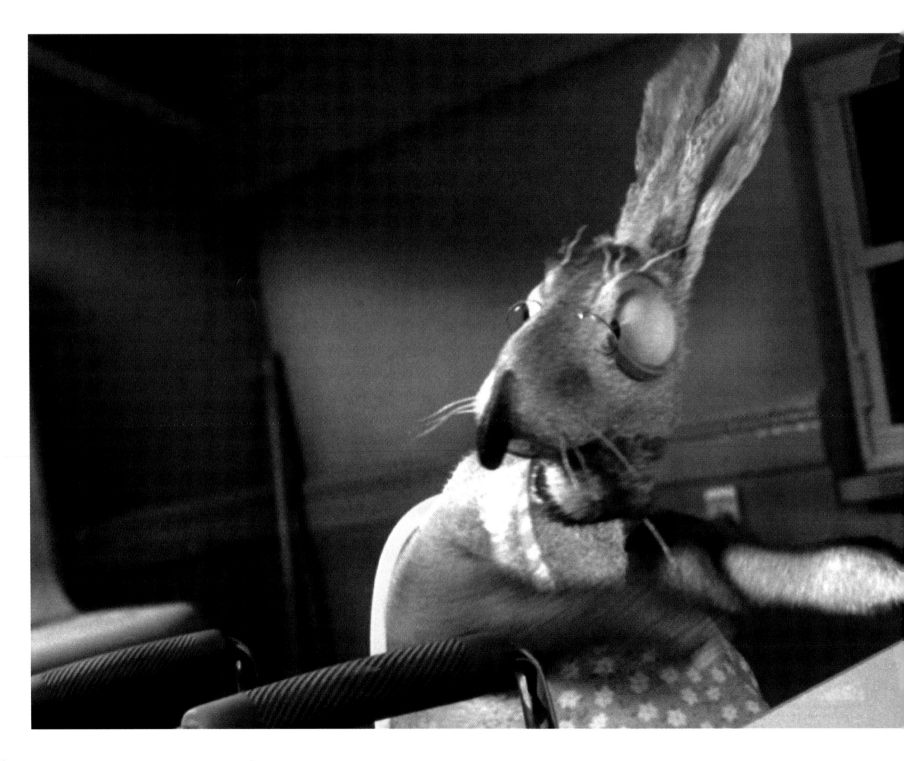

Bunny got up.
Was she awake, or was she dreaming?
She wasn't sure.

Bunny saw no cake inside the oven.
Instead, she saw the moth and a
bright light shining.

Bunny flew with the moth
into a world of stars and light.
As they flew, others joined them.
And Bunny joined her husband.